From an idea of Sasha Sagan

Tupag the Dreamer

by Kerry Hannula Brown • illustrated by Linda Saport

MARSHALL CAVENDISH • NEW YORK

Long, long ago, there was only one season all year long, the season of winter and of darkness. There was no such thing as sunlight; there was never any daylight.

In this time, there was a village on the shore of the ocean. Life was very hard for the villagers because it was always so dark. The villagers could only hope for enough moonlight and starlight to help them see when they went hunting for food. But even on the brightest nights it was difficult to see the whales, the walrus, and the fish they hunted, so often they had very little food.

For one villager, though, life was not very hard. His name was Tupag, and all day long, every day, he would only lie on the beach and daydream. The hunters would call to him as they pushed the umiak into the black-blue seawater, "Come, Tupag! Come join the hunt so that the village may find more food to eat."

But Tupag, snug in his warm parka and mukluks, would only shake his head. "Not today," he would reply. Then he would return to his dreams while the hunters shook their heads in dismay.

And when the villagers went off to search for the elusive moonlight berries that grew in niches and on knolls around the village, they would call to Tupag, "Come, Tupag! Come look for berries with us so that the village may find more food to eat."

But again Tupag would only shake his head and reply, "Not today." Then he would return to his dreams while the berry-gatherers shook their heads in disappointment.

While the hunters peered through the dark, shivering in the ocean's icy wind, they muttered, "That Tupag—what a lazy dreamer!" And while the berry-gatherers pushed aside the cold, wet snow looking for moonlight berries, they murmured, "That Tupag—what a good-for-nothing dreamer!"

Tupag, though, was very happy dreaming his dreams by himself as he lay on the shore. He dreamed that he could lie down in the midst of a forest of moonlight berries. "Not for me," he told himself, "poking my fingers into the snow until they're frozen just to find a berry here, two berries there." No, there would be so many berries that they would drop gently into his mouth. Plop! Plop! He would suck their juice and eat them by the dozens until his lips would be stained with the juice and the skins would stick to his mouth and teeth

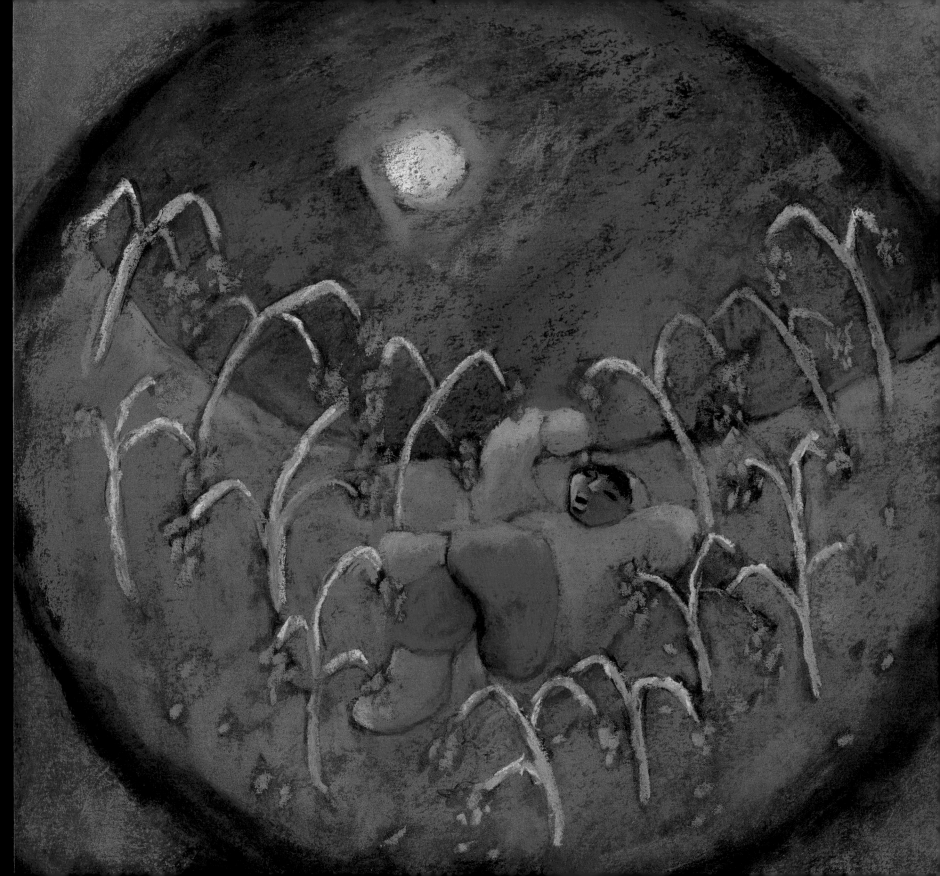

Or Tupag would dream that fish would fling them-
selves toward him so that he need only point his spear
and have it full of fish. "Not for me," he said, "poking
my spear a hundred times into the ocean water and
catching only one fish or two if I'm lucky." He would
catch salmon enough to eat until he was full at every
meal, all day long, not just sometimes if the moon was
full so the hunters could see better and catch enough
fish for all the villagers to eat their fill.

On days that were especially cold, Tupag would dream that the moonlight was as golden and warm as firelight. This was his favorite dream, but whenever he tried to tell the other villagers about it, they only laughed at him. "Tupag," they said, "it's bad enough that you're a lazy good-for-nothing, but now you're being foolish as well." Then they would turn their backs on him and walk away.

One day, as Tupag settled himself down to begin another day of dreaming, all the villagers gathered on the beach around him.

"Tupag," said one, "yesterday as we searched for food we talked about you a great deal."

"We decided," said a second, "that we are tired of feeding you. If you will not help us, you need to leave the village."

Tupag was very sad, but he knew they were right. Slowly he turned and left.

He walked away from his village and soon it disappeared into the darkness behind him. As he walked, he thought about the village he was leaving behind and the friends he would never see again. He tried to dream so he wouldn't feel so alone, but he was too sad. For once no dreams came to soften the bleak blackness around him. He saw nothing but scattered stars blurred by his tears and heard nothing save the noise of his feet crunching through the crust of the snow where no one had ever gone.

Suddenly, ahead of him, Tupag saw a shape that was blacker than the darkness around it. Curious, Tupag crept slowly closer. He called to the shape, "I am Tupag. Who or what are you?"

"Come closer," said the shape in a low hoarse voice.

Tupag felt a little frightened, but he crept closer and closer until he could see that the shape was actually a huge raven.

"You know who I am?" said Raven.

"Yes," said Tupag, "you are Raven, creator of the world."

"And you are Tupag, the lazy good-for-nothing," replied Raven very, very quietly.

"Yes," said Tupag, hanging his head in shame. "I am Tupag, the lazy good-for-nothing."

Raven fixed one black eye on Tupag, and Tupag felt so sorry for all his years of laziness that he wished with all his heart that he could sink through the snow and disappear forever.

"Tupag," said Raven. "Tupag, look at me."

Tupag trembled, but he raised his eyes to Raven.

"Tupag, you are lazy, but you are also a dreamer," said Raven gently. "I have been watching your dreams with you over the years, and I have enjoyed them greatly."

Tupag was surprised. Everyone else had always laughed at his dreams, yet Raven liked them!

"Thank you," said Tupag.

"Tupag," continued Raven, "everyone has his place. You must return to your village to take your place with the other villagers. And, as a sign that I have told you to return and as a reward for the years I have enjoyed your dreams, I will make one of them come true. Which one shall it be?"

Tupag thought and thought. Did he want forests of moonlight berries? Did he want fish to leap onto the fish spears? Suddenly, Tupag knew which dream should come true. All his years of dreaming had made him a wise thinker, and so he made the wisest choice. He whispered his choice to Raven, who nodded and almost seemed to smile.

Then Tupag turned to return to his village. He looked back over his shoulder, but Raven was gone, and there was only darkness stretching behind him.

Back in the village, Tupag called all the villagers together and told them what had happened.

"But, Tupag, which dream did you choose?" asked the villagers.

Tupag pointed to the sky. "One day, soon, we will see another moon. But it will be like a fire, with warm and golden light. It will light up all the land and it will stay as long as the darkness does every year. Its warmth will melt the snow and we will be able to find berries quickly and easily. Its light will show us where the animals are and we will be able to find many to eat so that we may have as much food as we want. We will even have enough to last us through the months of darkness."

"How do we know this is true, Tupag?" asked one villager.

Tupag pointed to another part of the sky and the villagers saw brilliant lights of blue, green, white, and gold floating across the sky like a giant sail. "There," said Tupag, "is Raven's sign. That is the promise of the season of light to come."

The villagers were so excited that they began to dance with joy until they moved as fast as the lights in the sky.

From that day on, Tupag was an honored member of the village. He became the village storyteller for, as the villagers said, "Everyone has a place, and Tupag's is to dream. He will share his dreams with us every night when we return from hunting and gathering berries, and during the day he will tell his stories to the children."

So, as the days of light grew longer and longer, life became much easier for the village. Everyone had so much to eat during the season of light that they saved enough food for the season of darkness, too. And no matter how cold or long the season of darkness seemed, the villagers knew that light would return to take its turn in the sky.

"Besides," Tupag would tell the children as they watched the winter's lights spiraling together like spinning flowers, "although life may be easier in the warmth of summer, the long darkness of winter is also good. After all, that is when we dream our dreams."

For Jamie, Shane, Ayla, Leisl, and Haley—
Who listen so well,
Teach so much,
And love so greatly.
—K. H. B.

For Gabriel
—L. S.

Text copyright © 2001 by Kerry Brown
Illustrations copyright © 2001 by Linda Saport
All rights reserved.
Marshall Cavendish, 99 White Plains Road, Tarrytown, NY 10591

Library of Congress Cataloging-in-Publication Data
Brown, Kerry.
Tupag the dreamer / by Kerry Brown; illustrated by Linda Saport.
Summary: A lazy man's daydreams delight Raven the creator who brings
the season of light to the man's cold, dark village.
ISBN 0-7614-5076-9
[1. Seasons—Fiction. 2. Eskimos—Fiction.] I. Saport, Linda, ill. II. Title.

The text of this book is set in 16 point Veljovic Medium.
The illustrations are rendered in pastels.
Printed in Hong Kong
First edition
1 3 5 6 4 2